By Lisa Banim
Based on the series
created by Terri Minsky

DISNEY
PRESS

New York

Printed in the United States of America

First Edition
1 3 5 7 9 10 8 6 4 2

Library of Congress Catalog Card Number: 2003112345

ISBN 0-7868-4635-6
For more Disney Press fun, visit www.disneybooks.com
Visit DisneyChannel.com

"**H**ey, Miranda, have you noticed anything *weird* in the halls today?" Lizzie McGuire asked her best friend as they joined the sea of kids flowing toward the cafeteria.

"Nope," said Miranda Sanchez. "Seems like the same old *weird* Hillridge Junior High crowd to me."

Lizzie frowned. Obviously, Miranda had failed to notice the lime green dragon standing in the doorway they'd just passed. It had been wearing a silver space helmet.

"No, really," said Lizzie. "You seriously didn't notice anything?" She started to point, but the dragon quickly disappeared into the crowd, dragging its scaly tail behind it.

"Notice *what*?" Miranda stopped and looked at Lizzie. "I know," she said, snapping her fingers. "You trimmed your bangs."

"Try again," Lizzie said as a large silver robot stepped right in front of them.

"Whoa," said Miranda. "What the heck is this? Wear a Bizarro Costume to Lunch day? I totally didn't hear *that* announcement."

"Maybe there's something going on that we don't know about," said Lizzie.

Miranda gaped as three creatures in green vinyl miniskirts and matching cone hats stepped out of the girls' room. "And maybe that's a *good* thing," she noted.

"Greetings, fair maidens," said Gordo, walking up to them. "Headed to ye olde midday banquet?"

Lizzie raised an eyebrow. *Fair maidens? Ye olde midday banquet?*

Okay, Gordo has either: (a) just stepped out of a time machine; (b) just finished a medieval crossword puzzle; or (c) just decided to join today's Club Weird. And it *better* be (a) or (b)!

"Um, sorry, Gordo," said Lizzie. "But Miranda and I are headed to *plain old lunch*. And so are you."

Gordo shrugged. "Whatever. I was just getting into the spirit of this *Knightscape* role-playing stuff that seems to be going on today."

"What's *Knightscape*?" asked Miranda.

As if on cue, two more weird creatures walked right up to them—a knight in a shiny silver space suit and some kind of robot princess wearing a metallic purple robe.

The two kids, whoever they were under their costumes, didn't seem to mind walking against Hillridge rush hour traffic. They were aggressively handing out pieces of paper to kids as they headed in to lunch.

The knight silently thrust a colorful leaflet into Lizzie's hands and kept walking. "Um, thanks," Lizzie said. "I think."

"What does it say?" Miranda asked. She peered over Lizzie's shoulder.

Lizzie frowned. "There's an emergency fan club meeting after school. For the TV show *Knightscape*."

"Oh, I get it now," said Miranda. "Thanks, but no thanks." She plucked the flyer from Lizzie's hand and sent it soaring into a nearby trash can. "*Geek*-scape," she whispered to Lizzie.

"Hey, *Knightscape* is a pretty decent show," Gordo said, overhearing her. "It's sort of a King

Arthur-in-space deal on the Galax-E Channel."

"Sorry, Sir Gordo," Miranda said. "But still no thanks."

"Don't you think maybe you're being a little narrow-minded?" challenged Gordo. "I bet you've never even watched a single episode of *Knightscape*."

"That's because I have a *life*," Miranda told him. "A *non*-geek one."

Lizzie tensed. Miranda was looking seriously annoyed—and so was Gordo.

Guys! Hello? You're best friends and you're fighting over a TV show! Time to tune in to *reality*!

"Hey, is anyone else starving?" Lizzie said brightly, hoping to break the tension. "*I* sure am. Come on, guys."

Lizzie walked quickly around the corner, into

the doorway of the large cafeteria—and straight into a card table with a green sign that read SAVE KNIGHTSCAPE!

Behind the table sat a girl wearing a glittery green mask and a cone hat. That weird green dragon with the space helmet stood beside her.

"Good morrow," the masked girl said in a tiny voice. "Hast thou come to aid in our mission? Please help." She pushed a clipboard across the table toward Lizzie.

"Um, help?" Lizzie said, confused.

Just then a tall girl wearing a green sorceress mask appeared beside the tiny-voiced girl. Two sparkly silver antennae wobbled atop the sorceress's green foil wig and tall cone hat.

"You!" the ugly sorceress thundered at Lizzie. "Play your part in destiny!"

Lizzie jumped back. "Destiny?" she squeaked. The costume was intimidating enough without the girl inside it—whoever she was—coming at her like the Wicked Witch of the West.

"Let's get out of here, Lizzie," Miranda whispered. "Like, *now*."

"Wait a minute," Gordo said. He threw Miranda an annoyed look. "I want to find out what's going on. What's the deal?" he asked the girls in costume.

Lizzie glanced around the cafeteria, which was filling with Hillridge students. Luckily, no one was paying much attention to the *Knightscape* table near the doorway—or to anyone who happened to be standing next to it.

Not *yet*, anyway.

Attention! Back away from the table. i repeat, back away from the table—or face your eternal geek destiny!

Just then, Larry Tudgeman rushed up to Lizzie and her friends. He was dressed as a king in a long, velvet robe and a cardboard crown. He carried a clipboard and a tinfoil sword.

"Have you heard the news?" he asked anxiously. "*Knightscape*, the most incredibly creative and inspiring science-fiction television series of all time, is being *canceled*!"

"Gee, too bad," Miranda muttered. "Can we get some food now?"

Lizzie nodded. Then she gasped and nudged Miranda. Ethan Craft, the cutest and most inspiring *guy* of all time, was entering the cafeteria. And strutting right beside him was Kate Sanders, Hillridge cheer queen—and reigning mean queen. Claire and a few of Kate's other stuck-up friends trailed behind them like a posse-in-waiting.

"Ohmigosh!" Miranda whispered to Lizzie. "Ethan and Kate are going to see us here, by the geek sign-up table! We're doomed."

Gordo, meanwhile, had failed to notice the imminent social disaster. "Tudgeman," he said, putting a hand on Larry's shoulder, "you have my sincerest condolences. *Knightscape* was a classic."

"*Is* a classic," Tudgeman corrected. "For weeks now, our noble fan club has been petitioning the Galax-E Channel to bring back the show and save its worthy characters from oblivion. Today we bring our quest to Hillridge. Wilst thou sign?" He held out the clipboard.

"Well, sure," Gordo said, taking the clipboard. He signed the petition and handed it to Miranda.

"Right," Miranda said, scribbling her initials. "Here, Lizzie. Sign. *Quick.*"

As Lizzie took the clipboard, she glanced back over her shoulder. *Uh-oh.* Ethan and Kate were just a few steps away. But that wasn't the worst part—

Kate had just locked eyes with her. "Ohhh, look!" she cried, loud enough for everyone to hear. "It's a geek costume party! What are *you* doing, McGuire? Signing up for Dork Court?"

2

Lizzie gulped.

Thanks to Kate, almost every kid in the cafeteria—including Ethan Craft—was now staring at her.

This is *not* the way I wanted to get Ethan's attention, Lizzie thought.

Kate gave Lizzie her she-beast sneer. Then she said, "Getting ready to blast off for Planet Geek?"

Lizzie cringed. She felt completely stupid, and completely paralyzed, unsure of what to do next.

We interrupt this broadcast to bring you a special bulletin: Kate Sanders is on a mission to infect the galaxy with a virus identified as Noxious Snob. Beware, Hillridge, the disease is seriously incurable.

Ethan stood staring at the strange *Knightscape* costumes. "Too weird," he said—but unlike Kate, he sounded fascinated instead of critical.

"*Totally* weird," Claire added—and her tone was totally superior.

Miranda tugged at Lizzie's sleeve. "Lizzie, let's go," she said.

Lizzie tried to push the petition clipboard away, but the ugly sorceress suddenly stopped her. With her big, green face and star-topped antennae, the sorceress loomed over Lizzie. "Sign!" she demanded.

Lizzie smiled weakly. "S-sorry," she said, glancing back at Ethan. "But I've really got to go right now. Um, maybe later?"

"Just sign the petition, Lizzie," Gordo advised in a low voice.

The sorceress drew herself up to her full height. She pointed a gem-ringed finger at Lizzie. The large emerald flashed under the cafeteria's fluorescent lights. "Mordella commands you to sign!" she said. "Or suffer your fate!"

"Awesome," Ethan said, suitably impressed with the show.

"Oh, *puh-leez*," Kate said with snobby disgust.

Lizzie looked from "Mordella"—whoever she was—to Kate and wondered which fate was worse: facing the Queen of Geeks, or the Queen of Mean?

I'm totally trapped, Lizzie told herself. She opened her mouth to answer, but felt herself collapsing into nervous giggles instead. "I must *escape*!" she blurted out. "From *Knightscape*!"

Then she started to laugh even louder. Now kids were *really* staring. Even Kate looked confused.

"Hey, good one, Lizzie!" Ethan said.

Lizzie stopped mid-giggle. Wow, she thought. Ethan actually thinks I'm *funny*!

Number One Thing Guys Say They Want in a Girlfriend: a great sense of humor. That's me! i'm clever! i'm hilarious! Move over, Jim Carrey!

Pumped by Ethan's praise, Lizzie whirled back to Mordella. Wiggling her hands over her head to imitate the sorceress's antennae, Lizzie said, "Look out, Mordella! I'll get you—and your little dog, too!"

Mordella's shoulders slumped, but Lizzie hardly noticed. She was totally focused on Ethan. He was smiling at her brilliant impersonation of the Wicked Witch of the West. Even Kate was speechless.

"Hey, Lizzie, you look like you're doin' that funny dance move," Ethan said. "You know the one—"

He wiggled his hands over his head, imitating a music video that a group called the Freaky Dudes had made famous.

"'I'm a freaky-freak, freaky-freak,'" Ethan sang. "'I'm freaky-freaky!'"

Lizzie joined in. "'I'm a freaky-freak, freaky-freak . . .'" she sang happily. "Look at me . . . I'm super freaky . . ."

"That's a fact, McGuire," Kate quipped. Then she turned on her platform sandals and stalked toward the lunch line. The popular kids followed, still laughing.

"Later, Lizzie," Ethan called over his shoulder with a friendly wave and a dazzling smile.

Thrilled, Lizzie turned back to her friends. "Did you see that smile?" she squealed.

Miranda and Gordo looked at each other. "Uh, yeah, Lizzie," Miranda said. "I think *every-one* did."

Lizzie suddenly realized that her friends weren't laughing. Neither were the members of the *Knightscape* fan club.

The princess was staring down at her petition clipboard on the table. The dragon had slumped into the chair beside her. And the sorceress didn't seem quite so tall now. She was wiping her eyes under her mask.

Oh, no, Lizzie thought. I've hurt this poor girl's feelings, whoever she is. But I was just *joking*!

"Gee, um . . . Mordella?" she began. "I'm really—"

But the ugly sorceress didn't give her a chance to finish. She ran out of the cafeteria, with the princess right behind her.

"Might as well get some grub," Gordo said. "I don't think they're coming back."

"I guess that Wicked Witch thing wasn't a

good idea," Lizzie said to her friends as they headed toward the lunch line. "But I was only joking . . . you know, goofing on the weird costume. Everyone knows that, right?"

"Maybe," Gordo said. "Or . . . maybe not. These people take this fan stuff pretty seriously."

"*How* seriously?" asked Lizzie.

"Well, they're usually very attached to the characters they choose to role-play," explained Gordo. "Some of them even see their costumes as extensions of their identities."

Now Lizzie felt *really* bad.

"Don't worry, Lizzie," Miranda said. "*We* know you didn't *mean* to totally destroy that poor girl's universe."

"Thanks," she told Miranda. "That helps a lot."

All that was left on the lunch line was cold mock pizza, or as Gordo called it, "English muffin à la cheese-covered dog food." But Lizzie didn't feel like eating anyway. Especially when she saw the SAVE KNIGHTSCAPE! posters tacked up all over the cafeteria. There was even one over their table.

Lizzie sighed and sipped halfheartedly at her carton of apple juice. Then she noticed Larry Tudgeman sweep by, still wearing his crown and robe.

"Larry," she called, "can you come here a sec?"

The Tudge turned back. He bowed before Lizzie and swept out his hand, nearly dropping the lunch tray he held in the other. "At your service, my lady," he said.

Lizzie bit her lip. Obviously, Tudgeman hadn't heard yet about the Wicked Witch incident. "Um, who were those kids in costume at the door?"

Tudgeman adjusted his crown. "Oh, that was my loyal and obedient daughter Princess Glenndar and the great and powerful Mordella, the most feared sorceress in all of *Knightscape*."

"Ooh-kay," Miranda muttered. "Now we're getting somewhere."

"No, I mean, who *are* they, you know, like in *real* life?" Lizzie asked.

King Tudgeman looked confused for a minute. "Oh," he said finally. "Right. Mordella is our fan club president, Audrey Albright. The princess is her best friend, Mavis Donnelly. And the dragon, Brutivere, is really Sir Julian of Far Pluto. Mordella cast a spell on him."

Lizzie stared at Tudgeman. He'd done it again. "The dragon is *who*?" she asked.

Earth to Planet Tudge! Earth to Planet Tudge! is *reality* beyond the realm of Larry?

"Oh . . . uh, right," said Tudgeman. "That would be Stuart Kent. He's Audrey Albright's boyfriend and the Hillridge fencing team captain. My competition. On the fencing team, I mean. Not for Audrey's affections or anything like that."

With a flirtatious smile, Tudgeman added, "I'm still very available in case an interested fair maiden, such as *yourself*, was wondering."

He's kidding, right?

Ignoring Larry's waggling eyebrows, Lizzie silently recited the names he'd mentioned: *Audrey*, *Mavis*, and *Stuart*. Although she didn't know any of these kids personally, Lizzie definitely knew *about* them.

Without her sorceress costume, Audrey Albright had enormous glasses, very pale skin, and pale blue eyes. She wore her long, rarely combed dark hair past her waist. Audrey was famous for supporting major geek causes, like the recent "Silence is Golden" campaign for the school library.

Mavis Donnelly was tiny and blond and very, very quiet. She attended Lizzie's Spanish class, but she rarely said *hola* to anyone except Audrey's "Dragon Man" boyfriend, Stuart Kent, who sat beside her. Lizzie had hardly ever seen—okay, *noticed*—Stuart without his fencing mask, except in Spanish.

Just then, Mavis appeared at the table and leaned close to Lizzie's ear. "I hope you're happy, Lizzie *Too-Cool* McGuire. Audrey's bawling her eyes out in the girls' room. All because of YOU."

"Oh, no!" Lizzie cried, jumping up from the table. This was all a misunderstanding. She was going to apologize to Audrey right now!

"Lizzie, wait!" Miranda called, but Lizzie tore out of the cafeteria. Everything is going to be fine, she told herself as she hurried down the hall to the girls' room. Lizzie figured she'd just tell Audrey how sorry she was and that would set everything right.

She threw open the door and burst into the lav. The place was empty.

Then Lizzie noticed something that sent a chill right through her.

There was a message written on one of the mirrors in green gel. It read:

GOOD-BYE, MORDELLA.
FOREVER.

CHAPTER

3

In horror, Lizzie stared at the girls' room mirror. "'Good-bye, Mordella. *Forever.*'?" she whispered. "What is *that* supposed to mean?"

Had Audrey written the creepy message as a farewell tribute to her *Knightscape* heroine? Or had Audrey meant something else?

"Audrey?" Lizzie called.

No answer.

"Mordella?" Lizzie tried again. She checked under the stall doors, just in case. No pointy green sorceress shoes.

The girls' room door burst open. "I knew I'd find you in here," Miranda said breathlessly. "Did you talk to you-know-who?" She jumped when she saw the goopy green gel on the mirror. "Gross. What *is* that stuff?"

Lizzie glanced back at the mirror. The gel was dripping down the glass now, making the message look even scarier.

"Mordella's gone," Lizzie told Miranda. "For real."

"Maybe she blasted off on her rocket-powered broomstick," Miranda said.

Lizzie frowned. "Miranda, be serious. I have a really bad feeling about this. And it's all my fault. Do you think Audrey did something drastic? That she ran away or something?"

"Lizzie, that's crazy," Miranda said. "She's probably on her way to her next class right now."

"Or maybe—" Lizzie gulped. "—she was kidnapped."

Miranda checked Lizzie's forehead. "No temp, but, uh . . . are you feeling okay?"

"I'm fine," Lizzie sighed. "I just hope Audrey is." She pointed at a spot on the tile floor. "Look, green gel. There's another glob by the window."

"Looks like Audrey was taking off her sorceress makeup in a hurry," Miranda said. "I mean, wouldn't you?"

"Well, yeah," Lizzie said. "But it definitely looks like Audrey's gone AWOL."

Miranda slid down to the lavatory floor tiles, waving her arms in the air. "Aaaaaaaah!" she cackled. "I'm melting . . . melting . . . into a puddle of evil goo!"

"Miranda, come on. I know I started it, but *enough* with the *Wizard of Oz* jokes," Lizzie said. "We need to find Audrey right away. I *have* to apologize to her so Mordella will come back."

Miranda unmelted herself. "Sorry, Lizzie," she said. "I'll help you find Audrey, okay? But like I said, she's probably in class. Like *we* should be right now. Hello? Home Ec?"

"Right," Lizzie said. "You go ahead and I'll be there in a second. I need to make a quick check around here for clues. Just in case."

"Okay," Miranda said with a shrug. "At least I can honestly tell Ms. Wilkerson that you're in the girls' room."

After Miranda left, Lizzie looked carefully around the lavatory. She checked out every stall and peered under every sink. When she spotted a tiny trail of silver sparkles, she followed them to the window ledge.

The girls' room window was the kind that had a hinge on top and swung outward. Lizzie found it unlocked and open a crack.

Lizzie pushed at the glass, swinging it farther out. Then she stuck her head through, checking under the window.

The girls' room was on the ground floor, so it would have been easy enough to climb out and jump to the ground. And the bushes lining the building would have been good cover for sneaking away.

So, thought Lizzie, Audrey *could* have snuck out of school without being spotted by the door monitors.

Just then, the bell rang. Lizzie lurched back and the window's heavy glass swung down.

"Yow!" she cried.

An ugly bump began to rise on Lizzie's forehead, but she didn't have time to think about that right now. Late students really annoyed Ms. Wilkerson. And the teacher didn't like excuses—even good ones.

Really, Ms. Wilkerson, once the FBI hears about my work on this case, they'll totally give me a late pass.

Lizzie stepped out of the girls' room. The hall was empty—except for Audrey Albright's boyfriend, Stuart Kent.

He must know where Audrey is, Lizzie told herself, striding up to him.

Stuart was no longer wearing his dragon costume. He stood at his locker, struggling to pull out his big fencing-equipment bag.

"Hi!" Lizzie said brightly. "You're Stuart, right?"

Stuart jumped about ten feet. "Uh, yeah," he said. "Hi."

Lizzie gave him a big smile. "Do you by any chance know where Audrey's next class is?" she asked.

"Um . . . Audrey?" Stuart ran a hand through his curly, bright red hair. "I dunno."

"I'd really like to talk to her," Lizzie added quickly. "I'm Lizzie McGuire. We're in the same Spanish class and—"

"I know who you are," Stuart said, shutting his locker. "I sit behind you."

"Um, right," Lizzie said, flushing. "Sorry. Anyway, did you happen to see Audrey after lunch?"

Stuart turned around. "Yeah. I mean, no." He hesitated. "Maybe. Look, I said I dunno, okay?"

Whoa, thought Lizzie. Why is Stuart acting so jumpy? He sounded almost . . . *guilty*.

But he's Audrey's *boyfriend*, Lizzie told herself. What would he be guilty of?

Just then, Lizzie spotted Mavis near the water fountain across the hall. She was watching them with interest. And she definitely did not look happy.

Stuart saw Mavis, too. "I, uh, I gotta go," he told Lizzie quickly.

"Stuart, wait!" Lizzie said as he brushed past her. "It's an emergency. I really, really need—"

Mavis quickly walked up. She put an arm on Stuart's elbow and told Lizzie, "You're going to make Stuart late for his fencing match. Haven't you caused *enough* trouble today?"

"Look, I just wanted to tell you guys that I'm sorry for that little misunderstanding back in the cafeteria," said Lizzie. "I'm sure *Knightscape's* a great show, and—"

"Come on, Stuart," Mavis said, cutting Lizzie off. She started pulling Stuart down the hall. "Let's go. Larry's already in the gym warming up."

"Please tell Audrey that I'm sorry," Lizzie called.

But Mavis and Stuart just ignored her.

Lizzie slumped against the wall of lockers. Obviously, Audrey's friends were not going to be very cooperative.

Fine, Lizzie told herself. I'll just have to solve the mystery of the missing she-geek without their help.

4

I am *not* overreacting, Lizzie assured herself as she hurried to Home Ec. There was that creepy message on the mirror. And the girls' room window was open with sparkles on the ledge.

But maybe there was some other reason Audrey had gone to the window, thought Lizzie. Like maybe Audrey felt sick and was trying to get some fresh air.

That's it, thought Lizzie, stopping dead in the hallway. If Audrey felt sick, then she wouldn't have reported to her next class. She would have gone to the nurse's office instead.

"Which is exactly where I'm going," mumbled Lizzie with an about-face turn.

The best thing to do, she decided, was just pretend she wasn't feeling well. The sick act would not only give her a chance to find Audrey and apologize, it would also give her a valid excuse for being late for Ms. Wilkerson's class.

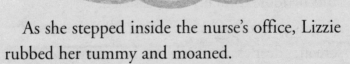

McGuire, you're looking like a genius. Now all you have to do is look like a genius with a stomachache!

As she stepped inside the nurse's office, Lizzie rubbed her tummy and moaned.

But the "I'm gonna hurl" act was totally wasted. Nurse Richards wasn't there. The little sign on her desk with the smiley face thermometer said BACK IN A JIFFY!

Fine, Lizzie thought. Time for a quick detective sweep. Softly, she called, "Audrey?"

No answer.

Lizzie noticed the folding screen at the far side of the room. She heard someone shifting on a cot behind it.

Aha, thought Lizzie. She crept up to the screen. Then she moved her head around the edge to get a look at the patient sitting back there.

"Aargh!" cried the patient.

"Aargh!" cried Lizzie.

The patient wasn't Audrey. It was cute Danny Kessler from the wrestling team. He sat on the cot with an ice pack on his knee—in his boxers! And he looked totally embarrassed.

"Sorry, Danny!" Lizzie cried. She grabbed the screen, desperate to hide her flaming face. Unfortunately, the screen had wheels. It slid halfway to the other side of the room. Then it collapsed around Lizzie like a cloth-and-metal accordion.

"Ow!" Lizzie squawked.

"Hey, Lizzie, are you okay?" Danny called.

"I'm fine," she replied, her voice muffled under the screen. *Just terminally mortified,* she added to herself.

"Oh my goodness, what have we here?" a voice cried. Lizzie felt the screen being lifted.

Nurse Richards stared down at Lizzie. "I can see you're going to need an ice pack, dear," she said. "For that bruise on your forehead."

Lizzie sighed. The bruise on her forehead was from the girls' room window. The bruise on her *knee* came from the screen.

Detective work sure can be hazardous, Lizzie decided as Nurse Richards pulled her to her feet.

Fifteen minutes later, Lizzie was limping down the hallway, ice pack—and late pass— in hand. Now she could be sure of two things. One: Audrey wasn't hiding in the nurse's office.

And two: She could never face Danny Kessler again.

On her way to Home Ec, Lizzie passed the art room. The class was filled with kids painting sets for the school musical, *Camelot*.

Hmm, thought Lizzie. Audrey was pretty good with costumes. Could she be working on the play?

It was worth a shot, Lizzie decided. Especially since she already had a late pass.

She opened the door, and looked around. The art teacher wasn't in the room, and Lizzie figured she was making a run to the supply closet. Excellent, thought Lizzie. Here's my chance!

"Excuse me," she called loudly, "I'm looking for—ahhh!" Lizzie ducked when a flying paint sponge nearly hit her in the face.

"Oops," said a chunky girl in overalls. "I *missed*."

"What!" cried Lizzie. "You mean you were actually *aiming* for me?"

"That's right," said the girl, hands on her hips.

"We heard how you made fun of Audrey, Lizzie McGuire. You're not all that, you know." She dipped another sponge into the paint and looked at Lizzie threateningly.

Lizzie backed away. "I'm trying to find Audrey," she explained quickly. "I want to tell her I'm sorry. It was all a terrible mistake."

The girl raised one eyebrow. "Yeah?" she said. She put down the sponge. "Well, Audrey's heading up props for *Camelot*. She's supposed to be here to help. But she hasn't showed, which isn't like her. Audrey's never late. In fact, she's usually early."

"Thanks," Lizzie said. "I'll keep looking."

She left the art room and limped as fast as she could to Home Ec. Ms. Wilkerson pursed her lips, but she accepted the late pass.

Miranda had already mixed up the fake fudge she and Lizzie were supposed to make. "Five boxes of confectioners' sugar," she said proudly. "Is that cool or what?"

Lizzie stuck her finger in the bowl and tasted

the batter. "Mmm," she said. "Good. What next?"

"I don't know," said Miranda. "Let's check the recipe."

"Hey, I preheated the oven for you guys," a girl named Harriet said.

"You did?" said Miranda, spooning the fudge into a pan.

Harriet was really good at Home Ec. In fact, she was one of Ms. Wilkerson's favorites—a straight-A student who hung out in a lot of the same circles as Audrey.

"No problem," said Harriet. "You're all set."

"Gee, thanks," said Lizzie. "That was really nice of you."

Harriet smiled. "Oh, anytime," she said, watching Lizzie pop the pan into the oven.

Phew. it's nice to know every last friend of Audrey's isn't out to get me.

As Harriet walked away, Lizzie and Miranda sat down at a table to talk.

For the next few minutes, Lizzie filled Miranda in on the bathroom search, the encounter with Stuart and Mavis in the hallway, getting the ice pack in the nurse's office, and the paint sponge incident in the art room.

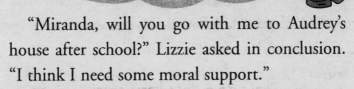

Okay, so i left out the part about seeing Danny Kessler in his boxer shorts. Can you blame me? it was way embarrassing.

"Miranda, will you go with me to Audrey's house after school?" Lizzie asked in conclusion. "I think I need some moral support."

"Lizzie, I really think you should just wait until tomorrow," Miranda said. "Audrey will get over it, already."

"I'm not so sure about that," Lizzie said. "Besides, it would be a nice thing—"

"Hey, what's that smell?" Miranda asked.

Lizzie sniffed the air and frowned. "Something's burning," she said. "Hey! I think it's our fudge!"

She rushed to the oven, but Ms. Wilkerson was already there, turning it off. The teacher removed the smoking tray and placed it in the sink, where it sizzled ominously.

Lizzie bit her lip and looked around the room. All the kids in the class were either laughing or coughing.

Ms. Wilkerson looked angry. "Just what did you two think you were doing?" she asked Lizzie and Miranda. "That oven was set on broil."

Lizzie and Miranda exchanged glances. "Um, sorry," Lizzie said. "I guess we got the temperature mixed up."

"I'll say you did!" Ms. Wilkerson cried. She threw her hands in the air. "One does not put no-bake fudge in the oven, ladies. That's why the recipe is called *no* bake."

Miranda groaned.

Behind Ms. Wilkerson's back, Lizzie heard a giggle. It was Harriet. She had already cut her unbaked fudge into perfect little squares and placed them on a plate.

"Want one?" she asked Lizzie with a smile.

Lizzie sighed. She and Miranda would have gone back to the recipe and read the directions—if Harriet hadn't rushed up to them offering a "preheated" oven.

So much for Audrey's friends letting me off the hook, thought Lizzie. By the end of the day, every geek at Hillridge is sure to hear some version of the Wicked Witch cafeteria incident and begin plotting some heinous revenge scheme.

There was only one way out of this mess, Lizzie decided. She had to find Audrey and apologize—fast!

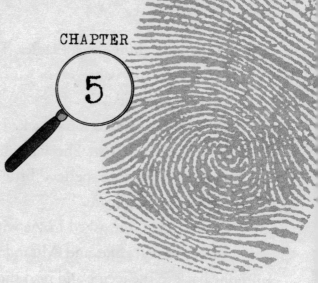

" I'm starving," Lizzie told Miranda when the last bell of the day rang. She'd been too upset at lunch to eat anything substantial. And their Home Ec fudge had been an inedible disaster. "Let's stop by my house for a snack before we head to Audrey's house, okay?"

"You really don't want to go over there, do you?" Miranda said.

Lizzie sighed as she shut her locker door. "Well, I'm not exactly looking forward to it," she said. "But I have to apologize."

"We could just skip it," Miranda said. "Talk to Audrey tomorrow when she shows up at school."

"You mean *if* she shows up," Lizzie corrected. She and Miranda waved to Gordo as they headed out of the building. He had a science club meeting till four o'clock.

Club meeting? thought Lizzie. She stopped short in the hall.

"Wait just a sec," she said. "Isn't there an emergency *Knightscape* fan club meeting after school today? That's what their flyer said. Audrey has to be there. She's the president."

"Nope," Miranda said. "It got canceled. Gordo told me because he was thinking about going."

"You're kidding," Lizzie said. "He didn't tell me that."

Miranda shrugged. "Guess he didn't want to remind you about the whole *Knightscape* deal," she said.

"As if I could forget," Lizzie said with a sigh.

"Well, Audrey must really be gone if the meeting was canceled."

"Guess so," Miranda said. "Hey, do you think your mom baked cookies today?"

"Maybe," Lizzie replied. But suddenly she wasn't so hungry anymore.

Sigh. You know the guilt is overwhelming when even chocolate chip cookies lose their appeal!

A short time later, the girls walked into the McGuire living room—and found a major war going on.

Lizzie's annoying little brother, Matt, and his two best friends, Lanny and Melina, were playing cards. Sort of.

"Lanny, that is *not* how you play Dragon Duels!" Melina said disgustedly. She threw her cards on the floor. "Don't you know anything?"

Lanny just grinned and gathered up all of the cards.

Matt checked the back of a brightly colored box. "No, Melina. Lanny's right. Two red dragons beat the purple one. It says so right here."

"Give me that!" Melina said, grabbing the box. "Well, no wonder. This is Dragon Duels *Gold*. Totally old school. There's a whole new version that blows this one away. Only little kids play Gold level now."

"Excuse us, little kiddies," Lizzie said. She and Miranda stepped over the Dragon Duelers on their way to the kitchen. "Enjoy your lame game."

Melina flipped her shiny, light blond hair. "I've won thirty bucks."

Miranda's eyes widened. "Really?" she asked.

Lizzie tugged her best friend's sleeve. "Cookies. In the kitchen. Free."

But as she pulled Miranda through the door, she heard Matt say, "Heeeeey, I've got a great idea! Maybe these Level Gold cards are worth some money—to the little kids who haven't gotten the scoop yet about the new version."

Lanny nodded vigorously.

Lizzie rolled her eyes. Matt's "great ideas" usually meant trouble.

"I see where you're going with that," said Melina. "And I know just where we can unload these worthless cards. At Fantasticon!"

"You mean that big sci-fi/fantasy convention downtown on Saturday?" Matt said. "Awesome! Melina, you're brilliant!"

Melina smoothed her pink pleated skirt and smiled. "Of course I am."

Lizzie shuddered and headed straight for the cookie plate on the kitchen counter. "That's the last thing I want to hear about right now," she told Miranda. "*Sci-fi* stuff."

After grabbing a couple of cookies and fruit bars, Miranda and Lizzie strolled out onto the deck.

"Ahh!" cried Lizzie, almost tripping over a strange, alien-looking being stretched out on the chaise lounge.

It was Lizzie's mom, wrapped like a mummy in hot towels. Cucumber slices covered her eyes and dollops of squashed avocado dotted her face.

"Um . . . Mom?" Lizzie asked a little nervously. "What's up with this?"

if it's true that girls grow up to be just like their moms, does this mean i'm doomed to become a veggie salad? Help!

Mrs. McGuire sat up, sending her slices of cucumber rolling across the deck. "Oh, hi, girls," she said brightly. "How was your day at school?"

Lizzie and Miranda exchanged glances. "Fine," they said in unison.

"I'm trying this amazing Queen for a Day spa home treatment," Mrs. McGuire explained. "I heard about it on TV. Today was the grand opening of Mud & Stuff. You know, that super-exclusive spa at the mall?"

"Sorry, Mom," Lizzie said. "Never heard of it. But it looks—" She struggled for the right word. "—interesting."

"Well, I popped right over and bought the kit," Mrs. McGuire went on. "The spa does the actual mud version at the mall, but the home kit uses fruits and veggies, so you can do it yourself. Much more economical."

"Um, right," Lizzie said, nodding. "That's really . . . great."

Miranda was speechless. She was staring at the avocado on Mrs. McGuire's face. It was turning from green to brown. *Yuck!*

"Gotta go, Mom," Lizzie said quickly. "We have to work on a . . . project."

"Oh, okay, sweetie," she said. "Just hand me those cukes, would you?"

Lizzie retrieved the wayward cucumber slices

from the other side of the deck. Mrs. McGuire put them back over her eyes. "Well, have fun."

Lizzie and Miranda hurried out of the McGuire Spa and over to Audrey's house. Lizzie had already written down the Albrights' address from the Internet yellow pages in the school library. Their phone number wasn't listed.

As they turned onto Audrey's street, a sleek green Jaguar came squealing around the corner. It stopped right in front of the Albrights' house.

A blond woman wearing a chic red pantsuit hopped out of the sports car. She was talking on her cell phone as she juggled shopping bags and boxes.

"Wow. Is that *Audrey*'s mom?" Miranda whispered in disbelief.

"I guess so," Lizzie said, still staring. So much for that girls-turn-into-their-mothers notion.

Audrey's mom might drive a Jag the color of Mordella's costume, but she looked *nothing* like the ugly green sorceress.

"May I help you, girls?" the sleek blond woman called to Lizzie and Miranda. She clicked off her cell phone with a long, manicured red nail.

"We're, um, friends of your daughter's," Lizzie said. "I mean, sort of. I mean, we'd like to be."

The woman looked confused. "My *daughter*?"

"You know, Audrey?" Miranda asked. "Blue eyes, big glasses, really long dark hair . . ."

Lizzie nudged her friend. "Shh," she said.

Chic Woman waved a shopping bag breezily.

"Oh, *Audrey*," she said. "She's not my *daughter*. She's my niece. I'm Audrey's Aunt Phoebe."

"Oh," Lizzie said.

"I stay with Audrey sometimes when her mom travels on business," the woman explained. "Her dad lives in Albuquerque, you know."

Aunt Phoebe's cell phone rang again. "Oh darling, *hello*!" she gushed as she answered it. "Hold on just a moment." She turned back to Lizzie and Miranda expectantly. "Yes?"

"We were just wondering whether Audrey was home," said Lizzie quickly.

Aunt Phoebe shrugged. "Oh, I have no idea," she said. "Last I heard she was going to the library after school." Then she threw them a fake, red-lipstick smile. "The poor child practically *lives* there. I'll tell her you stopped by. Ta-ta!"

Waving her leopard gloves at Lizzie and Miranda, Aunt Phoebe carried her bags into the house, still talking on her cell phone.

Yikes. **This woman's as synthetic as press-on nails. if i were related to a person like this, i'd live at the library, too!**

"Wow," Lizzie said. "It sounds like Audrey's aunt doesn't pay any attention to her."

"Girls, yoo-hoo!" Aunt Phoebe suddenly called after them. She clicked back down the steps of the porch in her designer heels. "I have something for you."

"Maybe it's a message from Audrey," Lizzie told Miranda eagerly. She ran and met Aunt Phoebe halfway across the lawn. Miranda followed.

Audrey's aunt unsnapped her alligator clutch. "You'll love this," she said. She handed Lizzie two cards for the Mud & Stuff spa.

"Um, thanks," Lizzie said.

Aunt Phoebe gave them another big, fake smile. Her teeth looked whiter than bleached bone.

"Remember, ladies, beauty is everything," she said. Then she peered at the girls more closely. "Mmmmm," she said with a critical frown. "Well, all is not lost. You should be happy to hear we're having a two-for-one special right now. See you *both* soon!"

"Geez," Miranda said to Lizzie after Aunt Phoebe disappeared into the house. "Can you believe Audrey is related to someone like *that*?"

"Maybe that's another reason why Audrey would want to disappear," Lizzie said. "Now I'm really getting nervous. That woman seemed totally distracted."

"What are you getting at?" asked Miranda.

"Just that she totally wouldn't notice if Audrey ran away," said Lizzie.

"C'mon, Lizzie. Do you think she'd notice if Audrey *never* came back?"

"Miranda, don't even joke about a thing like that!"

"Okay," Miranda said. "Maybe not *never*."

Lizzie sighed. "I'm just saying that if Audrey left a note saying she's spending the next two nights at a friend's house or something, I'll bet good ol' Aunt Phoebe wouldn't even check up on her. So if she did run away today—like I'm beginning to think she did—I'm guessing Aunt Phoebe might be too busy to even notice until the weekend."

"Yeah," Miranda said, nodding. "I guess I'd have to agree. It's entirely possible Audrey's aunt could lose track of her pretty easily."

"So, you can see why it's even *more* important now that we find Audrey," Lizzie said. "We have to let her know we care."

"We do?" Miranda asked.

Lizzie frowned at her friend.

"Just kidding," Miranda said quickly.

"We'd better check the library before it closes,"

Lizzie said. "It's worth a shot, anyway. Come on, let's go."

The girls hurried toward the Hillridge Public Library. As they got closer to Main Street, Lizzie saw SAVE KNIGHTSCAPE! posters everywhere.

"We're hot on your trail, Mordella," whispered Lizzie.

A powerful sorceress is no match for a clever detective! (As long as there's none of that Harry Potter wizard stuff involved!)

But as Lizzie and Miranda rushed into the large library's lobby, they came to a skidding stop.

"Which section?" Miranda asked. "She could be anywhere."

"Science Fiction and Fantasy," Lizzie said.

"We're not just looking for Audrey. We're looking for Mordella, too, remember?"

The girls split up in the paperback stacks. Miranda took the Fantasy aisles. Lizzie took Science Fiction.

The books were covered in heavy dust. *"Kerchoo!"* Lizzie sneezed loudly.

"Silence!" a voice whispered sharply.

"Sorry," Lizzie said, sniffling. "I couldn't help it."

A girl stepped out of the shadowy stacks. But she wasn't tall and dark-haired. She was small and blond. And she did *not* look pleased to see Lizzie.

"What are *you* doing here?" Mavis asked Lizzie. Her voice was very soft, but she still sounded annoyed.

Lizzie sighed. Princess Glenndar's attitude was becoming seriously tiresome.

"I'm trying to find Audrey," Lizzie replied. "Remember?"

"I'll give you a hint," Mavis said. "Mordella is *definitely* not here."

"So you *do* know where she is," Lizzie said.

"No," Mavis said. "I don't."

She turned to go, but just then Miranda appeared behind her. "Come on, Mavis," Miranda said. "Give Lizzie a break, okay? She just wants to apologize to Audrey. She's really, really sorry for hurting her feelings."

Mavis didn't answer.

Lizzie tried a different approach. "You know, I saw Mordella's message in the girls' room." Lizzie waited for Mavis's reaction.

The blond girl didn't flinch. "That's so interesting, Lizzie," she said, as cool as one of Mrs. McGuire's facial cucumbers. "Now, *vamos*. I don't want to talk to you about Audrey."

"Okay, Mavis, that is IT!" Miranda exploded in exasperation. "DO YOU KNOW what happened to Audrey or Mordella or whoever she is— or NOT?"

Like magic, the silver-haired librarian swept in. She picked up a "Silence is Golden" bookmark from a nearby table and held it up to Miranda.

"Oops," Miranda said. "Sorry."

The librarian nodded and walked away.

Lizzie frowned. That bookmark looked exactly like the ones from Audrey's "Silence is Golden" campaign at Hillridge's school library. Was Audrey starting a campaign at the *public* library now? Or had she actually been around somewhere in the Sci-fi section and dropped one of her own bookmarks?

Whoa, thought Lizzie, I need to ask that librarian about Audrey.

"Excuse me!" Lizzie called loudly, momentarily forgetting about the quiet rule. As her voice echoed through the book stacks, Lizzie suddenly remembered and cringed with embarrassment.

The librarian didn't say a word. She simply frowned and pointed to the door. Mavis smiled triumphantly.

Lizzie tried to talk to the librarian one more time, but the woman was now adamant in her pointing.

"I warned you once," she whispered. "Out. And I mean *now*."

MEMO
TO: Audrey Albright
FROM: Lizzie McGuire
SUBJECT: Silence
is Golden
Congratulations. i get it.

Lizzie and Miranda quickly left the library.

"I am *not* through with that Mavis," Lizzie vowed to Miranda. "Trust me on this one."

"Okay, so what's the new plan, detective?" asked Miranda as they descended the library steps.

"Back to Audrey's house," Lizzie said. "We need to talk to Aunt Phoebe again. I'll tell her that Audrey wasn't at the library, and I'm worried about her."

But when the girls reached the Albrights, the green Jaguar was gone from the driveway. And no one answered the doorbell.

"Maybe Audrey is here and she's not coming to the door," Lizzie said.

"Yeah," said Miranda. "She could be crying her eyes out in her bedroom."

"Gee, thanks for making me feel *sooo* less guilty," Lizzie said.

"If you ask me, Princess Glenndar is the guilty one," Miranda said. "That girl is definitely hiding something."

"Mmmhmm," Lizzie replied. She gazed up at the second-floor window of the house. There was a rope fire-escape ladder dangling from it. "What did you say about Audrey hiding in her *bedroom*?" she asked Miranda pointedly.

Miranda looked up at the window, too. "Oh no. Uh-uh. No way," she said. "We are *not* going to do this."

"Yes we are," Lizzie said. "That has to be

Audrey's bedroom. I'm just going to take a peek."

"Isn't that, like, illegal or something?" Miranda asked.

"No," Lizzie said. "Matt spies on people all the time. *He's* never been arrested, right? Come on, give me a boost."

Miranda sighed and interlaced her fingers to make a step. Lizzie put the toes of her left foot on Miranda's hands and lunged for the end of the rope ladder.

"Ow!" Miranda complained.

Lizzie reached again for the dangling rope. "I've almost got it," she said.

Just then, a dog began to bark in the next yard.

"Miranda," she said, "does that sound like a very *large* dog?"

"How should I know!" complained Miranda. "What do I look like? A dog-bark-sizing expert?"

Lizzie concentrated harder on grabbing the rope.

"N-nice doggie," Miranda groaned. "W-what a sweet d-doggy you are. Lizzie, I can't hold you much longer!"

"I've almost got it," Lizzie told her.

Just then, the dog gave a long, low growl.

"Hurry up, Lizzie!" cried Miranda. "I don't like the sound of that dog's growl."

Lizzie finally grabbed the rope and scooted up the ladder. She peered inside the window.

The room was empty. But it was Audrey's, all right. There were *Knightscape* collages and posters all over the walls. One of the posters was for a fan club rally, but Lizzie couldn't read the fine print.

"Please don't let that doggy's chain break . . . please, oh, please, oh, please," Miranda chanted. Then she let out a high squeal. "Eek! Lizzie, that dog's left its yard. It's coming our way! Hurry up!"

Lizzie quickly dropped to the ground, falling hard on her backside.

"Lizzie, are you okay?" Miranda said, rushing over to her friend.

"Y-yeah," Lizzie said. She was now staring down the nose of the tiniest, scrawniest dog she'd ever seen. It looked like a rat wearing a little pink coat.

Great. I bust my butt to save my best friend from Cujo the killer Doberman and it turns out to be Fifi the French rodent!

"Shoo," said Lizzie. "Go home."

The mini dog scampered away, wagging its ratty tail.

"Well, I think we've safely established that Audrey *isn't* home," Miranda said. "Can we please do something fun now? It's almost dinnertime."

Lizzie sighed and rubbed the seat of her jeans.

She was going to have another bruise for sure. Suddenly, she felt something in her pocket.

It was Aunt Phoebe's card for the Mud & Stuff spa. The spa was at the Hillridge Mall. And Miranda was definitely getting cranky.

"Hey, Miranda, I've got a great idea," Lizzie said. "Let's call Gordo and meet him at the mall. We can grab some pizza or something."

"Now *that's* a plan," Miranda said. "Time to take a *break* from your big case. Okay, Slavedriver Sherlock?"

"Right," she told Miranda, patting the card in her pocket.

And, of course, Miranda doesn't *need* to know that a good detective (like me) *never* takes a break!

"It sure feels great to be in a *normal* place again," Miranda said to Lizzie. "No more angry she-geeks. No more *golden* silence."

"Just giant fruit," Lizzie said loudly, over the pounding mall music. She took a flyer from a person in a huge banana costume. The leaflet had a discount coupon for a banana-papaya facial at Mud & Stuff.

Can't wait till Mom tries that one, Lizzie told herself.

She stuffed the flyer into her jeans pocket,

next to Aunt Phoebe's card. She was dying to check out the spa right away and talk to Audrey's aunt again. But she had to be patient and do it carefully. Miranda might freak if she figured out they were still working on the Case of the Missing She-Geek.

"Where are we meeting Gordo?" Lizzie asked.

"At the entrance to the food court," Miranda said. "Look, there he is!" She waved. Gordo waved back. He was leaning against a kiosk with a familiar sign. Lizzie recognized it right away. It was the same *Knightscape* fan club poster she'd seen in Audrey's bedroom.

"Greetings, damsels," Gordo said as Lizzie and Miranda walked up. "Woudst thou havest pizza, tacos, or sushi?"

"*Ixnay* on the chivalry, Gordo," Miranda said. "Tonight we're having the geek-free special."

Lizzie stepped closer to the *Knightscape* poster. "Aha!" she said. "Today is Thursday, right?"

Miranda and Gordo nodded.

"Okay," Lizzie said. "If Audrey doesn't show up at school tomorrow, and I still can't pin down Aunt Phoebe, then I'll bet Mordella shows up at the convention center on Saturday."

"Huh?" Miranda said.

Lizzie pointed to the poster. "Ta-da! You are invited to the most Fan-tastic sci-fi convention in the galaxy—Fantasticon!"

"Cool," Gordo said. "You mean we're going? All of us?"

"Absolutely, positively *no way*," Miranda said, crossing her arms. "Lizzie, have you lost your mind? We are not going to risk our social reps by attending a full-blown Geek-a-thon."

"Look at it this way," Lizzie said, "it's the chance of a lifetime to go where you've never gone before."

Miranda rolled her eyes.

Just then, a tall, dark-haired girl about their age with her hair cut to her chin in a trendy bob walked toward them. She was wearing a black leather miniskirt, long dangly earrings, and high black boots.

"Whoa," Gordo said.

The girl kept walking and bumped straight into Lizzie, sending her flying against the Fantasticon sign.

"You're blocking the aisles," the girl said meanly. Then she rolled her heavily lined green eyes and added under her breath, *"Geeks."*

Speechless, Lizzie, Miranda, and Gordo watched the girl walk off.

"Did you hear what she called us?" Miranda said, stunned. *"Geeks!* Just because we were looking at this stupid poster. See, Lizzie? I told you this sci-fi stuff is totally geek-o-rama. Our social lives will be ruined forever if we go to that convention!"

"Well, we may not have to go," Lizzie said. "Hopefully, we'll find Audrey before Saturday. But if we do go to Fantasticon, we can do it undercover. You know, in costume."

"I'm okay with that," Gordo said, shrugging.

Miranda covered her eyes. "Aaargh! This is the worst idea you've ever had, Lizzie. And you've had a *lot* of them."

"It's for a good cause," Lizzie reminded her. Then she added quickly, "You know, since we're already here at the mall, we *could* stop by Mud & Stuff and talk to Aunt Phoebe. If we find Audrey before Saturday, then no Fantasticon."

Miranda uncovered one eye. "Okay," she said. "Deal."

Psych! Miranda never even suspected that i brought her here to keep working the case. i am *so* good!

Lizzie, Gordo, and Miranda headed straight to Mud & Stuff.

"Uh, do you mind if I wait outside?" Gordo

asked, looking in the window of the salon. He saw hanging plants, bowls of fresh fruit, and an espresso machine. "This isn't really a guy kind of place."

Miranda grabbed his elbow. "Oooh-no, Gordo," she said. "You're coming with us. Just so you can see how it feels to risk *your* social rep."

Miranda was only half kidding—until she, Lizzie, and Gordo walked all the way into the salon, and Lizzie gasped in horror. "Cheer-Queen alert," she whispered.

Before they could back away, Kate Sanders looked up from a manicure table. "Oh, look!" she said to Claire and half a dozen cheerleader friends. "It's the three Geek-a-teers!"

Train wreck! Code blue! We need help here. STAT!

"Oh, great," Miranda said to Lizzie under her breath. "Kate and her Poisonous Posse."

The Queen of Mean strutted over with the rest of her court trailing behind her.

"Hey, Lizzie," said Kate, "I heard about what happened in the nurse's office today. How you were falling all over yourself trying to sneak a peek at Danny Kessler—" She giggled nastily. "—when he was in his boxer shorts."

Kate's friends laughed. And Lizzie felt her face begin to flame.

This is one of those rare, special moments, when you really need the floor to open up and swallow you. Come on floor, just think of me as a piece of fried chicken.

"McGuire, you are so weird," Claire said.

"Yeah," said Kate. "She's pathetic."

Miranda and Gordo just stood staring at Lizzie. "Tell us that isn't true," Gordo said.

"Yeah," said Miranda. "She's lying, right? I mean, you mentioned the nurse's office, but you didn't mention anything about Danny Kessler. I would have remembered that."

"Well . . . I did surprise Danny," Lizzie tried to explain. "And he was in his boxers. But it was all an *accident*."

"But it *did* happen," Kate declared.

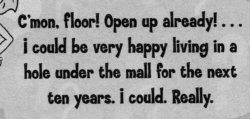

C'mon, floor! Open up already! . . . i could be very happy living in a hole under the mall for the next ten years. i could. Really.

This just may possibly qualify as the most

mortifying moment ever, Lizzie decided. Time to beat a hasty retreat.

Seeing a spa employee washing mud off her hands in a sink against the wall, Lizzie hurried through the salon, leaving her friends and the cheer queens staring after her.

"Excuse me," Lizzie asked the woman in the black Mud & Stuff uniform. "Is Phoebe here right now?"

The woman shook her head. "Sorry, you just missed her. She left for a business dinner. I'm the assistant manager. May I help you? We have a special on our Waldorf facial scrub today. That's raisins and walnuts and—"

"No thanks," Lizzie said with a sigh.

As she headed back to Miranda and Gordo, Lizzie decided that Aunt Phoebe was as hard to catch as her niece. But Detective Lizzie McGuire was a long way from giving up!

When Lizzie got home from the mall, Matt was on the front steps. He was pacing back and forth and rubbing the back of his neck.

"Good. You're home," he said when he saw her.

"That's sort of obvious, isn't it? What do you want?" said Lizzie tiredly.

"Your opinion," said Matt. Her spiky-haired little brother thrust a handful of Dragon Duels cards in front of her face. "Tell me the difference between these four cards," he demanded. "I'll give you a hint. One of them is *not* like the others."

Lizzie looked at the cards. All four had dragons on them. Three were gold. One was silver.

"Is this some kind of trick?" she asked suspiciously.

Matt shook his head. "Nope."

"Okay, the one on the right is silver," Lizzie said. "Duh. What do you think I am, six years old or something?"

"Exactly!" Matt said. "I figured that you, my sister of very little brain, could provide me with the perfect level of valuable market research."

"Get your dragon breath away from me, Fossil Hair," Lizzie said. She pushed past her annoying brother and ran upstairs. She needed to do some research of her own—on the Internet.

She sat down at her desk and turned on her computer. The screen flashed and glowed.

Where should I go first? she wondered. After a moment's hesitation, she typed in a web search for the Fantasticon site.

This quest is not without perils.
Evil cookies could be planted in my computer
to monitor my track through Dork Land. i
could be spammed with action-figure
e-deals and sci-fi newsletters for years to
come. On the other hand, who cares?
i never met a cookie i didn't like.

Lizzie had never been to a sci-fi convention in her life. But she needed to solve this case soon— and save Mordella.

Er, *Audrey*, she corrected herself.

She checked out the Fantasticon events schedule. Special guests, art shows, discussion panels, gaming, costume contests . . . the list was endless.

The phone rang just as Lizzie clicked on the *Knightscape* link. Lizzie answered.

"Hey, Lizzie," Gordo said.

"Hi, Gordo." Lizzie's eyes were still scanning

the screen. "I'm online, doing some research for Fantasticon."

"Me too," Gordo said.

"You know, the *Knightscape* logo is actually pretty cool," Lizzie said. "I like the astro-knight riding on the horse made of stars."

"That's the constellation Pegasus," Gordo said.

"Really?" said Lizzie. "That's sort of clever."

"I like the jousting aliens game," said Gordo. "You can play against other *Knightscape* fans online."

"Wait a minute," Lizzie said. "You mean you've been on this Web site before?"

Suddenly, a Mordella icon appeared on the screen, looking greener and uglier than ever.

"Eek!" Lizzie cried.

The sorceress image cackled loudly and then disappeared.

"Lizzie, are you okay? What's going on?" Gordo asked.

"Oh nothing," Lizzie said. "Mordella's head

just popped up, and it freaked me out. Guess I'm a little jittery."

"Speaking of jittery," Gordo said, "I know Miranda's not too cool with the Fantasticon thing, but I think it'll be pretty interesting."

"Yeah, well . . . we'll definitely need good disguises," Lizzie said.

"Leave that to me," Gordo said. "Getting three decent costumes in thirty-six hours won't be easy, but I'll look into it. I intend to squeeze some info out of the Tudge."

Lizzie sighed. "The convention might actually be bearable, but I sure wish we could find Audrey before Saturday. It would be a lot easier if I could just call her house, but the Albrights' phone number isn't listed. And even if it was, Audrey's aunt is so busy that I'm guessing I'd just get an answering machine."

"And if Audrey's there, she'd probably erase the message," Gordo added.

"Exactly," Lizzie said. "Then again, if Audrey's

there, then she's probably okay, and I'll see her in school soon enough."

"I guess you're sort of stuck," Gordo told her. "I mean, you can't exactly spend the night camped out on the Albrights' front porch. And you don't know if Audrey's really missing yet, either. That'd be pretty serious if she was."

"I know," Lizzie said. "I just hope she's at school tomorrow."

Lizzie sighed. She knew Gordo was right. She had no real evidence that Audrey was in trouble. But still . . . Lizzie knew that if there was even the most miniscule chance that something had happened to Audrey, she would never, *ever* forgive herself.

Mordella! Audrey! Come out, come out, wherever you are!

The next morning, Lizzie caught up to Miranda and Gordo in the school courtyard.

"Have you seen Audrey anywhere?" Lizzie asked them.

"Well, she isn't sitting at the geek table," Miranda said, craning her neck.

"And I grilled Tudgeman at the bus stop this morning," Gordo added. "He has no idea where Mordella is. In fact, he thinks it's pretty cool he gets to be acting president of the KFC while she's missing in action."

"Um, KFC?" Lizzie asked.

"*Knightscape* Fan Club," Gordo said. "If you ask me, the Tudge is getting a tad power hungry. He refused to give me *any* info on costume stores. He just kept saying true fans *make* their own costumes."

As they passed the cheerleaders' table, Lizzie saw Kate introducing a new student.

"Everyone, I want you to meet Cheryl Andrews," Kate announced loudly. "A really good friend of mine. She's new here at Hillridge."

"Hi, Cheryl," the cheerleaders chorused.

"Oooh, nice ring," one of them added. "Is it real?"

"Of course," Cheryl said. "It's an emerald. I never take it off."

Lizzie did a double-take. Cheryl was that trendy girl with the short dark hair, black leather miniskirt, and black boots who had meanly bumped into her at the mall the day before!

"Keep moving," Lizzie told Miranda and

Gordo in a low voice. She ducked her head and tried to walk quickly past the popular table, but it was too late. She distinctly heard Cheryl say the word "geek."

Was she talking about me, Lizzie McGuire? Or was she referring to geeks in a general sense? Lizzie wondered. There was no way to tell.

Whoa. This snobby Cheryl person is giving me a whole new perspective on the Hillridge Geek Society. Guess you really don't know how someone else feels until you walk a few halls in their sorceress shoes.

Today was Friday—and Lizzie's last chance to find Audrey before tomorrow's sci-fi convention. "I'm going to have to double my efforts on this case," Lizzie murmured to herself in home-room.

Even though Lizzie, Miranda, and Gordo had asked around in the courtyard, no one had seen—or admitted to seeing—Audrey anywhere since lunch the day before.

But Lizzie did speak to a girl who gave her a good lead. She said that Audrey often helped out Mrs. McKenzie, the school secretary, during homeroom.

"This is my big break," Lizzie whispered to Miranda. "I can check the office right now. Either (a) Audrey will be there, (b) Mrs. McKenzie will know where she is, or (c) I'll know Audrey is out for sure."

"Sounds a little risky," Miranda said. "I mean, that's Principal Tweedy's office. *Yikes.* How are you going to get in there?"

"No problem," Lizzie said. *I hope,* she added silently.

As soon as their homeroom teacher had

finished taking attendance, Lizzie raised her hand and asked for a pass to the main office. "I need to, um, call my mom about my . . . orthodontist appointment," she fibbed.

Miranda grinned and gave her a thumbs-up. Lizzie was usually a lousy liar.

So what if i don't wear braces anymore? Kids always say they have orthodontist appointments. it's, like, the universal excuse.

The teacher raised an eyebrow, but she gave Lizzie a pass anyway. Lizzie breathed a sigh of relief.

When she got to the office, Mrs. McKenzie wasn't sitting behind her desk—Cheryl Andrews was! She was answering the phone, taking calls from parents about absent students.

The dark-haired girl stared meanly at Lizzie

with her piercing green eyes. "You again," she said to Lizzie. "What do you want, geek?"

Lizzie's mouth dropped open. What was this girl's problem?

"Why do you keep calling me a geek?" asked Lizzie. "I'm *not* a geek."

Cheryl shrugged and twirled a pencil, showing off her expensive emerald ring. "Whatever you say. *Geek*."

Before Lizzie could answer, Mrs. McKenzie bustled in. Cheryl smiled sweetly at the secretary.

What a two-faced witch, Lizzie thought, frowning. Just like Kate.

Wow, i can see why this girl is fitting in so well with the Queen of Mean and her crew. They love phony more than rats love cheesy.

"Thank you for being such a dear and taking

those messages," Mrs. McKenzie told Cheryl. "You were right. I really did need a little break. I'll take over now."

Cheryl smiled again and got up from the desk. The phone started ringing off the hook. As soon as Mrs. McKenzie was busy taking calls, Lizzie said, "So, Cheryl, how come you're helping out in the office on your first day at Hillridge? Shouldn't you be meeting people and stuff?"

Cheryl snorted and reached for a compact in her purse. She flipped it open to admire her ivory complexion, then dabbed powder over a small shiny spot on her nose. "I think I know everyone I want to know already."

Okay, this is where I hurl that oh-so-clever comeback. One that will leave Cheryl reeling before she hits the floor. You know, the old one-two knockout punch. Like, um . . . uh . . . well . . .

"Really," Lizzie said.

Still looking in the compact's mirror, Cheryl fluffed her perfect bob. "But since you're so nosy . . . I was in here getting my schedule and Mrs. McKenzie said she was shorthanded today. She needed someone to fill in for just a minute."

Cheryl snapped the compact shut, and added, "The regular student office helper geek is absent."

Aha! Lizzie thought. So Audrey *is* absent!

When Cheryl breezed out of the office in her pink miniskirt, Lizzie pretended to make that phone call to her mom. "Orthodontist appointment," she mouthed to Mrs. McKenzie.

The secretary smiled and waved. "Oh, the orthodontist. Don't worry, dear. You'll get those braces off soon and your teeth will look absolutely beautiful."

Lizzie smiled back, keeping her mouth tightly shut. She hated lying. But she was determined to find some sort of lead on Audrey—

As she glanced down at the notepad on the

desk, she saw it. Yes! Cheryl had left the absentee list in Principal Tweedy's "in" basket. But Audrey Albright wasn't on it!

Darn! thought Lizzie.

Lizzie whirled around to ask Mrs. McKenzie about Audrey. But the secretary had stepped away to copy an armload of standardized test forms.

That's when Lizzie noticed the student files behind the counter. They were all alphabetized.

Glancing around nervously, Lizzie looked under A for Albright. She jotted down the private home number on a notepad and quickly put the file back. Then she dialed the phone, trying to reach the Albright home.

"I've got you now, Audrey," whispered Lizzie.

But no one answered.

Where was the missing she-geek?

11

At lunch, Lizzie bravely approached the geek table. Alone.

She didn't want to. She had to. There was no other way to get the 4-1-1 on Fantasticon and bring back Mordella. Her only hope was to throw herself at the mercy of Larry Tudgeman.

King Tudge was holding court—literally—at the table, still wearing his *Knightscape* crown. He pounded his tinfoil scepter on the floor and announced, "The Hillridge KFC emergency strategy meeting is now in session."

"Um, Larry?" Lizzie asked. "Can I see you for a minute?"

Tudgeman sat up straighter. "How darest thou interrupt? Canst thou not see I am busy?"

"Sorry," Lizzie said. "But it's really, really important."

"Well, this meeting is important, too," Tudgeman said, adjusting his cape. "Tomorrow we go into battle."

"Battle?" Lizzie asked.

"To save *Knightscape*," said a juggler in a polka-dot space suit.

"We're staging a fan club rally at the Fantasticon convention," added a courtier with braids wound around her head.

"Larry, I just have a quick question," Lizzie said. "But I need to see you in *private*."

All of the guy geeks hooted. "Way to go, my lord," one of them said to Larry.

Lizzie rolled her eyes. "It's about Mordella," she said.

Everyone at the table fell silent. "Very well," King Tudgeman said, rising. "I will grant the fair lady an audience."

Audience? Yikes! The whole cafeteria is watching me beg a dork in a cardboard crown to talk to me. Welcome to the Hillridge Junior High School Matinee. Six bucks, please, Theater One. Enjoy the show.

Tudgeman followed Lizzie into the hallway outside the cafeteria. "Okay," he said, "what's the deal on Mordella? Spill it."

"Actually, Larry, I'm trying to find her," Lizzie said.

"Mordella is fated to disappear, but the

Golden Sorceress will emerge to save *Knightscape*," Tudgeman said. "It's predicted in the Prophecy."

"What's that?" Lizzie asked. She didn't like that whole line about Mordella being "fated to disappear."

Tudgeman sighed. "You wouldn't understand. The *Knightscape* world is vast and deep."

"Well, I *want* to understand it," Lizzie said. "Really fast. I'm going to Fantasticon tomorrow."

"You will need a guide," Tudgeman said, crossing his arms. He looked off into the distance like George Washington crossing the Delaware.

"Um, right," Lizzie said. "Larry, will you help me? Um . . . please?"

Tudgeman thought for a minute. "I suppose," he said finally. "But on one condition."

Lizzie tensed. "What's that?"

"You will go as my queen."

Blecch! No way! Lizzie thought. But she had no choice. The geek underworld was going to be tough to negotiate. She definitely needed Tudgeman's help.

"Okay, Larry," she said with a sigh.

"The honor is mine, Queen Lizivere," declared King Tudgeman. He reached down and tried to kiss Lizzie's hand. She snatched it away.

"Not so fast," said Lizzie. "I'll need a costume. And two more for Gordo and Miranda. They're totally into *Knightscape* now, too."

Tudgeman gave a nod. "As you wish, my lady. It will be done." Then he bowed and swept back into the cafeteria.

Lizzie sagged against the wall.

There's no escaping it. i am *so* going to be tortured. Royally.

"OH, QUEEN LIZIVERE!" a voice called loudly.

Outside her Spanish classroom, Lizzie froze, then cringed.

Miranda and Gordo both turned to stare at her. So did everyone else in the hall.

Could Tudgeman possibly call *more* attention to this situation? ATTENTION ALL HILLRIDGE STUDENTS: LiZZiE McGUiRE iS QUEEN OF THE GEEKS!

Tudgeman took his sweet time walking up the hall toward Lizzie.

"Lizzie, what is going on here?" Miranda whispered.

"Long story," Lizzie said.

"We have time," Gordo said. "Look, Tudgeman's greeting his loyal subjects along the way with the royal wave."

Lizzie anxiously chewed her lip and waited for King Tudgeman.

"Your role as my queen begins immediately," Tudgeman announced to Lizzie when he finally reached her. "Your presence at my side is hereby requested for the Hillridge Fencing Finals."

Lizzie gulped. *Fencing?* Could this day possibly get any geekier?

"No!" Miranda whispered in horror. "Just say *no*!"

"My bout against Sir Julian of Far Pluto begins at two-twenty *sharp*."

Sir Julian of Far Pluto was *Stuart*, Lizzie

remembered, Stuart Kent, Audrey Albright's boyfriend.

And here he comes now, thought Lizzie, seeing the twitchy boy with curly red hair brush past her into Spanish. Quiet, blond Mavis followed, her small chin in the air. She didn't look at Lizzie.

Well, Lizzie told herself, at least I'll have a chance to keep an eye on those two.

"Sure, Larry," Lizzie replied.

He frowned and raised an eyebrow. "Excuse me? How didst thou address me?"

Lizzie cleared her throat. "I mean, yes, *my lord.* I'll be there."

"Lizzie, you have some serious explaining to do," Miranda said, as Tudgeman moved on.

"Yeah, what's with this *my lord* business?" Gordo asked, frowning.

Lizzie filled her friends in on her deal with the Tudge. They looked horrified.

"Hey, at least we don't have to worry about costumes now," said Lizzie brightly.

"Thanks, Lizzie," said Miranda. "But with what you have to go through, I'd rather wear a sack."

At two-twenty *sharp*, Lizzie took her place on King Tudgeman's bench at the Hillridge Fencing Finals. Mavis took her place on Sir Stuart's.

"Those two sure look cozy," Miranda whispered, leaning forward on the bleachers. She was sitting beside Gordo and right behind Lizzie. "Isn't Stuart supposed to be *Audrey's* boyfriend?"

Lizzie looked over at Sir Stuart's bench. Mavis was handing Stuart a little gold locket. He took it with a smile and put it around his neck under the vest of his fencing uniform.

"That *is* weird," Lizzie said, frowning.

Suddenly, Tudgeman appeared at her side. He had been warming up in the middle of the gym, showing off his fencing moves.

"Queen Lizivere, what willst thou give me as your token?" he asked, removing his face mask.

"Token?" Lizzie asked blankly.

"Something he can take with him into battle," Gordo said in a low voice behind her. "Like, a handkerchief or something."

"Um, I have some Kleenex," Lizzie said, hunting in her purse. She found a clean tissue and handed it to Larry. "Here you go."

"Throw it to me," Tudgeman said, as the buzzer rang to begin the bout.

Lizzie tossed the Kleenex. It fluttered to the floor in front of her. "Oops," she said.

But Tudgeman didn't seem to notice. He and Stuart were already facing off.

"Ohmigosh, are they really going to fight each other with those sword things?" Miranda cried.

"No worries," Gordo told her. "Those are foils, not swords. They have a spring-loaded tip. It's all electronic. The green light on the machine over there goes on when Tudgeman makes a hit. A red one means Stuart scored a point."

"Whatever," Miranda said, as the Tudge and

Sir Stuart began to dance around. "Johnny Depp does it better."

Lizzie wasn't watching the action on the floor. She was watching Mavis. The little blond sat in rapt attention. She cheered every time Stuart scored a point.

Whoa, was that actually a *smile* from the Ice Geek? Has Sir Stuart touched her heart? Could Princess Glenndar be . . . in love? On guard!

No way, Lizzie told herself. Mavis was Audrey's best friend. Stuart was Audrey's boyfriend. Which meant they were all very *friendly*. Right?

Then Lizzie noticed Stuart's Spanish textbook on the bench beside Mavis. There was something sticking out of it. A note! Could it be a message from missing-in-action Audrey?

Lizzie made a show of smiling and waving at Tudgeman when he scored another hit. So far, the score was tied.

"Miranda," Lizzie whispered, keeping her gaze on Tudgeman. "Over there. Spanish book. Note. Need it!"

"Gotcha," Miranda said. "Back in a sec."

Lizzie watched Miranda slip down from the bleachers and walk casually over to Stuart's bench.

Mavis's attention was totally focused on Sir Stuart. She didn't even notice as Miranda plucked the note from the pages of the book and returned to her seat.

"That was just too easy," Miranda said.

The referee stopped the action on the floor to explain his ruling on a point. The point went to Stuart. Half the spectators cheered. The other half booed.

"What does the note say?" Lizzie asked. "Is it from Audrey?"

"Well, it looks like a girl wrote it," Gordo said, frowning. "But it's in some kind of code."

"We'll just have to crack it, then," Lizzie said.

The next point went to Tudgeman. Lizzie smiled and waved. Tudgeman gave a little bow.

The buzzer rang to end the match. The Tudge was now king of the Hillridge fencing team. A gang of spectators ran onto the gym floor to congratulate him.

Mavis rushed to console Stuart.

"Come on, guys, let's get out of here," Miranda said. "Before King Tudge sees us."

"Just leave the code-cracking to me," Gordo told Lizzie, as they snuck out of the gym. He stuffed the note in his pocket.

Lizzie nodded. "Miranda and I will keep calling Audrey's house," she said. "*Someone* has to answer *sometime*."

One way or the other, she was going to solve the Case of the Missing She-Geek.

"Arrrgh!" Lizzie sat up in bed and threw her pillow at her alarm.

Eight A.M.

Today was Fantasticon, and she'd overslept! She and Miranda had called Audrey's house till ten-thirty when Miranda went home. All they ever got was a message saying the Albrights' answering machine was full. Then she'd been on the phone with Gordo half the night, trying to decipher the message from Stuart's text-book.

No luck all around. *Nada, nada, nada.* And now she'd overslept.

Nancy Drew didn't need an alarm clock. And even if she did, she'd never forget to set it. *Arrrgh!* At this rate, I'll *never* solve this case!

The phone rang. Lizzie hunted around for it on the nightstand, under the pillow. "Hello?" she answered finally.

"Good morning, sci-fi fan," Gordo said. "I've got Miranda on the line."

"He's cracked the code!" Miranda said. "You've got to hear this."

"Ohmigosh, that's so great!" Lizzie cried.

"It ended up being easy," Gordo said. "I found a link from the *Knightscape* Web site to some crazy fan page devoted to Knight*speak*. That's the official language of *Knightscape*. Anyway, the message was written in a mixture of Knightspeak and pig Latin."

"Incredible," Lizzie said. "But, Gordo, what does it say?"

He cleared his throat and read, "'Dear Sir Stuart, Please don't feel guilty about what we've done. It was meant to be. You and I were meant to be. What Audrey chose to do is her business. No one can blame us now. So just keep your mouth shut. Your devoted royal maid, Mavis.'"

Lizzie fell back against the mattress with the phone. "Whoa," she said. "Okay. So Mavis and Stuart know Audrey did something. Mavis says it's not their fault. Stuart *was* Audrey's boyfriend. But now it sure sounds like Mavis and Stuart are a couple . . . hmmm . . ."

Lizzie asked Gordo to reread the note one more time, hoping to hear some small clue.

When he got to the part that read, "No one

can blame us now," Lizzie suddenly cried out.

"Guys!" she said excitedly. "I figured something out!"

"Huh?" Miranda said.

"Audrey *did* disappear," Lizzie said. She jumped out of bed and began to pace the room. "But not because I hurt her feelings. I think Audrey was crying in the girls' room that day because of Mavis and Stuart!"

"Whoa," Miranda said.

"After that incident with me and Mordella in the cafeteria, I think that's exactly the moment Mavis chose to tell Audrey the truth about her and Stuart—that they were secretly in love and Stuart was breaking it off with Audrey."

"What makes you think that?" asked Gordo.

"Simple," said Lizzie. "That way, Mavis could tell all her geek friends it was *me* who'd made Audrey so upset. Then everyone would hate *me* instead of her!"

"Well . . . it's possible, I guess," Gordo said slowly. "Especially if Mavis already knew Audrey ran away—"

"Gordo," Miranda broke in. "I don't think it's just possible. I think that's exactly what happened. I mean, all along, I didn't think Lizzie's stupid goofing in the cafeteria was a big enough deal to send a girl over the edge. But the Stuart and Mavis thing—that *is* a big deal. Think about it. Audrey's best friend betrayed her with her boyfriend. Now that would be devastating to any girl. Lizzie, I think you are totally on the right track."

"Thanks, Miranda," said Lizzie.

"But what did Audrey *do*?" Miranda said. "Run away? Or . . . something worse . . ."

"We've got to try Aunt Phoebe again," Lizzie said, frantic. "Call you right back."

She hung up, then dialed the Albrights' number. The answering machine message came on again.

"Rats!" she cried. She called her friends back. "No luck at home. What next? I know! I'll try her Aunt Phoebe's salon."

"Lizzie," Miranda said, "the mall doesn't open for another three hours. You'll just get a recorded message."

"Yeah, you're right," said Lizzie.

"So . . . now what?" asked Miranda.

"Now we go to Fantasticon," Lizzie said firmly. "If we don't see Audrey there, we can at least confront Mavis and Stuart and find out what they know."

it's the oldest story in the book. The classic love triangle. Audrey loves Stuart, and Mavis loves Stuart, and Stuart loves Mavis. Kind of like, i love Ethan and Ethan loves . . . Okay, forget that last comparison.

"There's your king," Gordo told Lizzie an hour later. "Over there, by his dad's car."

Lizzie gazed across the convention center parking lot. "Uh-oh. He looks kind of . . . mad."

"Queen Lizivere, wherest hast thou been?" Tudgeman said as they approached. "You're late. And I have to set up the *Knightscape* booth."

"Sorry, my lord," Lizzie said. "Do you have the costumes?"

Tudgeman thrust a huge pile of sparkly gold, silver, and neon clothes and a full suit of futuristic knightwear into Lizzie's arms. "Here," he said. "I can't wait for late subjects. Put these on and I'll meet you at the *Knightscape* booth. Farewell."

Miranda looked down at the miniskirted gowns, elaborate eye masks, and large, pointy headware. "Gee, accessories too," she said.

Lizzie sighed. "Come on, guys, let's get this over with."

After Lizzie, Miranda, and Gordo had pulled their *Knightscape* costumes over their normal clothes, they headed across the parking lot.

"We look like freaks," Gordo said, walking stiffly in his plastic armor.

"We look like *geeks*," Miranda corrected.

"Well, we're supposed to," Lizzie said.

Just then, Lizzie was nearly bowled over by three small gold dragons making a beeline for the convention center. "There's something familiar about those dragons," she said, frowning. But she had no time to think about that now. She turned to Miranda and Gordo.

"Now remember," she said, "lips are zipped about Audrey in front of Tudgeman, okay? He and Stuart are big rivals, but they're also fellow geeks. We don't know who he might side with in this whole deal."

"Got it," Miranda said. Gordo nodded and made a lip-zipping motion.

They paid their ten-dollar admission at the

door and took the programs handed to them by a short, furry, rubber-footed hobbit.

The scene was overwhelming. Costumed characters from sci-fi movies, TV shows, and comics roamed the aisles. Music blared, and there were tables of vendors selling every kind of merchandise in the solar system.

There was also a card table run by three small dragons. They were doing a brisk business with a crowd of even smaller suited dragons.

Lizzie's eyes narrowed. Matt. Lanny. Melina. She was not going to even think about them right now!

"Okay, Detective Lizivere, wherest do we wander now?" Miranda asked.

"The *Knightscape* booth, I guess," Lizzie said. She looked across the convention hall. Tudgeman looked almost dapper in his dress crown and robes. Mavis and Stuart were there, too—holding hands under the table. *Blech.*

But no Audrey. Or Mordella.

"You know, the Hillridge mall should be opening soon," said Lizzie checking her watch. "I think we should try Aunt Phoebe's salon."

Lizzie dug into her jeans pocket under her silver-brocade miniskirt. She pulled out the Mud & Stuff business card and walked over to the public pay phones.

But when she looked down at the card to call the number on it, she froze.

"Look," she said to Miranda and Gordo. "Audrey's aunt's last name. It's *Andrews*. Phoebe *Andrews*."

"Yeah," Miranda said. "So?"

"That snobby new girl's name is Cheryl Andrews," Lizzie said slowly.

"Coincidence?" Gordo guessed.

"Cousin?" Miranda shrugged.

"No," Lizzie said. She broke through the crowd and ran toward the exhibit booths. "Mordella!"

CHAPTER

14

"I may be crazy," Lizzie told Gordo and Miranda, as she dashed across the convention hall. "But Cheryl just might be Audrey in disguise."

"What?" said Gordo. "No way."

"I know what you're thinking," said Lizzie as she moved through the crowd. "Cheryl is sophisticated and glam and acts just like Kate. She wears expensive makeup and has short hair and piercing green eyes. She appears to be nothing like Audrey with her frumpy clothes, geeky friends, superlong messy hair, pale blue blinkers, and big glasses—"

"Right," said Miranda. "They're practically complete opposites."

"But," said Lizzie, "Cheryl showed up just when Audrey disappeared. And Audrey is really good at disguises—like the Mordella costume. And, don't forget, we first spotted Cheryl at the mall—where Audrey's Aunt Phoebe could have given her a drastic makeover at her salon."

"Still, that's a pretty big leap, Lizzie," said Gordo as they passed a Star Trek fan booth. "Like to hyperspace."

"But it does explain why Cheryl was so nasty to me, for no apparent reason," said Lizzie. "If Cheryl had been Audrey all along, then she probably thought I had it coming for making fun of her Mordella costume in the cafeteria!"

"Lizzie, I think Gordo's right this time," said Miranda. "You're really reaching."

Lizzie kept moving. Her theory might be a long shot, but it was certainly *worth* a shot.

Take my advice: Be careful of the geeks you think you're passing on the social ladder because they may end up stepping on you before either of you reach the top. Ouch!

Lizzie ducked to avoid a collision with the tail of a Haley's Comet costume. Then she practically crashed into the Fantasticon accessories booth.

Miranda and Gordo were right behind her.

"Hey! Watch it, kids!" cried a tall green sorceress with an ugly mask and star antennae bobbing atop her green foiled wig and tall cone hat.

The sorceress glared at Lizzie and her friends. Her eyes flashed green—just like the green contact lenses in the booth's costume accessory case.

And just like the piercing green eyes of Cheryl Andrews! thought Lizzie. "Mordella!" she cried.

"I've got you now. Or should I say I finally found you, Audrey Cheryl Albright Andrews!"

Triumphantly, Lizzie reached out and yanked on the sorceress's green foil wig. The cone hat and sparkly antennae fell to the floor, and Lizzie stared at the person she'd just revealed—

The woman was about forty years old. With long, red hair.

"Oops," Miranda muttered, embarrassed.

"Whoa, Lizzie," said Gordo. "I told you, your theory was way off."

Lizzie's face flamed as she looked down at the crumpled foil in her hands. Then she looked back at the stunned woman.

Wow, thought Lizzie, I guess Gordo was right. She stooped down to pick up the hat.

"I'm so sorry, Mordella," said Lizzie.

"I know you are," said another voice.

Lizzie rose to find a spectacular golden sorceress stepping up to stand beside the woman in green. This new sorceress was wearing a dazzling long gown of gold—but flashing an *emerald* ring.

"That ring," whispered Lizzie. "I've seen it before on Audrey Albright *and* Cheryl Andrews."

Lizzie gulped as the newcomer removed her sparkly gold eye mask and said, "It is I, the Golden Sorceress—also known as Audrey Cheryl *Mordella* Albright Andrews."

"Amazing," Gordo said, sounding awed.

"Audrey!" cried Lizzie in extreme relief. "You're here. You're okay!"

"Of course," said Audrey. "I'm fulfilling the Prophecy of the Golden Sorceress."

"Prophecy?" Miranda said. "*What* prophecy?"

"I remember," said Lizzie. "Tudgeman told me something about a Golden Sorceress destined to save *Knightscape*."

"That's right," the red-haired woman said. "The Golden Sorceress reigns at last." She smiled at Lizzie. "I'm Denise-Marie Mathews, the actress who plays Mordella on the TV show. I'm retiring, so the show's writers are going to make Mordella disappear. She'll be vanquished next season. The Golden Sorceress character will be taking Mordella's place."

"You mean *Knightscape* isn't being canceled after all?" Gordo asked.

"No," Denise-Marie said, putting her green foil Mordella wig and cone hat back on. "Due to the efforts of all the show's loyal fans throughout the country—especially the Hillridge KFC—the network has agreed to another season."

"Wow," Lizzie said. "Congratulations, Audrey."

Audrey nodded. "Thanks, Lizzie." Then she lowered her voice and said, "Listen, Mordella and I are making the big announcement on stage in a couple of minutes, but can I talk to you alone for a second?"

"Absolutely," Lizzie said. "And I want to talk to you, too."

"We'll see you later then," said Miranda.

"Gordo and I will scope around a bit. Just for kicks," she added quickly.

Lizzie nodded. She had a feeling Miranda was actually *enjoying* Fantasticon.

"Come on," said Audrey. And Lizzie followed her to the snack bar.

Lizzie got a soda. Audrey got a fruit smoothie. Then the two of them sat down at a table.

"So, Audrey," Lizzie said, "here's the thing. I've been going crazy trying to find you. I'm really, *truly* sorry I acted like such a jerk in the cafeteria. I was trying to impress Ethan, and I didn't think about your feelings. I was totally wrong. And I'm totally sorry."

Audrey stirred her smoothie. "Thanks," she said. "And I have to say, I'm sorry, too. Cheryl was a little harsh with you."

Lizzie smiled. "Maybe just a *little*."

"Well, it's true. I was pretty upset about a lot of stuff," Audrey said.

"You mean about the Wicked Witch thing?"

Lizzie asked. "Or . . . Stuart and Mavis?"

"You know about that?" Audrey said, sounding surprised.

"Yeah, I do," said Lizzie. "That was a pretty raw deal for you."

"Yeah, it was," said Audrey. "Stuart and Mavis really hurt me. And I never saw it coming. I wrote that Mordella note on the girls' room mirror because I never wanted to be Mordella again. I was going to quit the KFC and anything having to do with Stuart and Mavis."

It must be terrible to be betrayed by your two best friends. Miranda and Gordo would *never* do anything like that to me. Gee . . . maybe i should start being a little more appreciative. Like, next time we order pizza, maybe i'll let *them* choose the topping.

"So I snuck out the girls' room window, left without telling anyone, and went straight to my aunt's spa," Audrey continued. "I got a makeover with the works."

"I knew it!" said Lizzie.

"You did?" said Audrey. "When?"

"Well, actually, I just figured it out a few minutes ago. At school, you really looked different," said Lizzie. "And acted it."

Audrey grinned at Lizzie. "Well, it took a *major* mud facial to give me this complexion, trust me on that. Aunt Phoebe was totally thrilled when she got to the spa and saw me finally changing my image. She even gave me her credit card and set me loose in the boutiques to buy a new wardrobe."

"And a new attitude," Lizzie pointed out. "You changed your whole identity. And frankly, Audrey, I don't think for the better."

"Yeah," Audrey said. "I guess I went a little overboard. But that geek-hater Kate and her posse showed up at Mud & Stuff while I was finishing up. They didn't even recognize me. But when one of the manicurists mentioned I was related to the spa's owner, Kate and her crew started being really nice to me. Big change from how they treated Audrey."

"But how exactly did you manage to become Cheryl?" Lizzie asked.

"It was sort of spur of the moment," Audrey said with a shrug. "When Kate asked my name, I just told them to call me Cheryl. It's my middle name anyway. And she just figured my last name was Andrews, I guess, because I told them my aunt owned the spa. I love games and costumes, so . . . you might say I played them."

"And me," Lizzie said. "It worked, too. Did you fool any teachers?"

"Didn't have to," said Audrey. "Before my classes, I told them I was going to start using my middle name, which they already knew from the attendance sheets. Then I just sat in the back instead of my regular seat. No one seemed to catch on. Or, if they did, they kept it to themselves."

"So that's how you did it," said Lizzie. "I wondered how Audrey Albright's name managed to stay off the administration's absentee list while all the kids kept telling me they hadn't seen you."

"I told you I'm good at games and disguises," said Audrey.

"That may be true," said Lizzie. "And you did look really different as Cheryl—really glam and everything—but I *liked* you better as Audrey."

"Me too," Audrey admitted. "I mean, I was so upset about Mavis and Stuart, I really didn't want to be Audrey anymore. But it only took me one day of hanging with Kate and her crowd to realize that trying to be someone you're not is just plain stupid. I hated it. My heart's in the *Knightscape* world and that's where I belong. Even if Stuart and Mavis are there, too. I'll just have to get over it."

"Yeah," Lizzie said. "Well . . . I'm just really glad you're okay. *Really.*"

"It was nice you cared enough about my feelings to keep looking for me, Lizzie McGuire," Audrey said. "And by the way, you're not really a geek."

"Thanks," Lizzie said. "I guess. But I'm not so sure what a real geek is anymore."

"Well, I'm cool now," Audrey said. "And you know *why* I'm cool? It has nothing to do with the way I look, or what I wear, or what I like. I'm cool because *I'm* finally cool with who I am."

Just then, there was a blare of trumpets from the small stage near the *Knightscape* booth.

"Gotta go," Audrey said, standing up and putting on her mask. "Time to fulfill the Prophecy of the Golden Sorceress. *Knightscape* lives!"

"Well, good luck," Lizzie said.

She watched as the Golden Sorceress made her way toward the stage. All the *Knightscape* fans bowed. And King Tudgeman looked as if he was in love. So did a lot of other guys.

Even Stuart and Mavis looked awed.

Audrey's their new action superheroine, Lizzie thought.

The Golden Sorceress suddenly looked back at Lizzie. With a flash of her emerald ring, she gave her a farewell salute.

The missing she-geek is no longer missing, Lizzie thought, saluting back. Not only that, she's just become the coolest geek in the galaxy.

"So," Gordo said to Miranda and Lizzie after the *Knightscape* announcement had been made and the cheering had died down. "Ready to go?"

"I guess it wouldn't be *so* bad if we stayed just a little longer," said Miranda.

Lizzie looked at her friend in shock. "Miranda, I thought you hated sci-fi geeks!"

Miranda shrugged. "Who knows? Underneath all that makeup, Styrofoam, and plastic, some of these guys could be kinda cute."

Just then, Lizzie and her friends were almost run over once again—by the three gold dragons.

Matt, Lanny, and Melina were being chased by a swarm of little kids. All the mini-dragons were demanding their money back.

"Ha!" Gordo chuckled. "Your brother and his fellow dragon sharks don't know it yet, but their troubles are just beginning."

"Why's that?" Lizzie asked.

"They invested all their profits into the new Dragon Platinum," Gordo explained. "But it was just announced on Stage Three that the level just moved up another notch."

"To SUPER platinum," Miranda added.

"Oh, my poor greedy brother." Lizzie laughed.

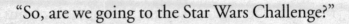

A mystery solved. A she-geek girl-power ending. And justice served. Life sure is sweet.

"So, are we going to the Star Wars Challenge?"

Miranda asked, looking at the Fantasticon events schedule. "Or the Galactic Highway video marathon?"

"Gee, I don't know, Miranda," Gordo said. He hid his face behind his laser shield. "If we're recognized, our reps could be blown!"

"Okay, okay," Miranda said. "So I overreacted."

"You can't live your life based on what other people think," Gordo said. "How many times have I told you guys?"

"A million!" Lizzie and Miranda cried together.

Miranda shrugged. "So we'll stay. It's cool," she said to Gordo.

Then she turned to Lizzie and whispered, "But let's keep our masks on anyway, okay? Just in case."

Lizzie McGUIRE MYSTERIES

Want to have a way cool time? Here's a clue. . . . Read the next Lizzie McGuire Mystery!

HANDS OFF MY CRUSH-BOY!

Lizzie has signed on for some truly grueling undercover work. Her crush-boy, Ethan Craft, is in major trouble at the Mr. Teen Hottie pageant. Someone is trying to wreck his chances of winning! To ferret out the fink, Lizzie's posing as Ethan's groupie. It's a tough job but *somebody's* gotta do it. (Added bonus: It'll seriously annoy Kate Sanders!)

"Ethan Craft, lots of cute guys, and a bizarro mystery? i'm all over it!"